Shadow's Baby

by Margery Cuyler
illustrated by Ellen Weiss

Clarion Books
New York

Clarion Books
a Houghton Mifflin Company imprint
52 Vanderbilt Avenue, New York, NY 10017
Text copyright © 1989 by Margery Cuyler
Illustrations copyright © 1989 by Ellen Weiss

For information about permission to reproduce
selections from this book, write to Permissions,
Houghton Mifflin Company, 2 Park Street, Boston, MA 02108.
Printed in the USA

Library of Congress Cataloging-in-Publication Data
Cuyler, Margery.
    Shadow's baby/by Margery Cuyler; illustrated by Ellen Weiss.
        p. cm.
    Summary: When Mr. and Mrs. Parker are expecting their first baby,
their dog Shadow is sure it will be a puppy.
    ISBN 0-89919-831-7
    [1. Babies—Fiction.   2. Dogs—Fiction.]   I. Weiss, Ellen, ill.
II. Title.
PZ7.C997Sh   1989   [E]—dc19   88-35257
                                            CIP
                                            AC

Y 10 9 8 7 6 5 4 3 2 1

Mr. and Mrs. Parker were expecting
their first baby.
"I hope it's a girl," said Mrs. Parker.
"I hope it's a boy," said Mr. Parker.

Shadow, the Parkers' dog,
was sure it would be a puppy.

Shadow wanted the puppy
to be happy.
He made it a soft bed
out of old rags.

He found the puppy some toys:
a ball, a rubber ring, and a stick.
He dug up a few bones and put them
next to the puppy's bed.

One evening, Mrs. Parker said,
"I think the baby's coming."
She went to the hospital.

Shadow stayed at home.
He waited.

And waited.

And waited.

Finally, after a few days,
the Parkers came back.
Mr. Parker was carrying a small bundle.
Shadow ran around in circles.
He jumped up and sniffed it.
It didn't *smell* like a puppy.

Mrs. Parker laid the bundle on the couch.
"This is our new baby," she said.
"Her name is Samantha."
Shadow looked at Samantha.
His tail drooped. She wasn't a puppy.
She was a little person.

He sniffed her again.
She smelled like sweet grass.

He licked her hands.
They wiggled like
tiny starfish.

He licked her hair.
It was as soft as feathers.
Samantha was small and
cuddly.
She was sort of like a puppy.
And she needed Shadow to
take care of her.

When Mrs. Parker put the baby to bed,
Shadow lay down beneath the crib.

At first, Samantha woke up every few hours.
"Waanh, waanh," she cried.
Shadow ran to Mrs. Parker and nudged her
with his nose.
"Time to feed her," said Mrs. Parker.
"She's crying because she's hungry."

During the next few weeks,
Shadow followed Samantha everywhere.
Sometimes, Samantha would grab Shadow's ear.
She'd shake it like a rattle.
Shadow would lean against her and let her pull
his ears as much as she wanted.

Shadow let Samantha splash him
when she had her bath.
One day, he licked her feet in the tub, and she smiled.
After that, she smiled every time she
saw Shadow.

When Samantha was six months old,
she got her first tooth.
She drooled on Shadow and his fur got wet.
Shadow just sat and let her drool
as much as she wanted.
"All babies drool when they get
their teeth," said Mrs. Parker.

A few months later,
Samantha tried to walk.
Shadow let her grab his tail
as she took a few steps.

Soon, Samantha could
walk by herself.

One day, Samantha said "Shaddy."
It was her first word, and it meant "Shadow."
"Now that she's learning to talk, it's time
to take her to the library," said Mr. Parker.

"And also to gym class,"
said Mrs. Parker.

"And maybe to swimming class,
too," said Mr. Parker.

From then on, Samantha was gone every morning.
Shadow would watch as Mrs. Parker put her
in her carseat.
Then he'd try to jump in the car.
"No, Shadow," said Mrs. Parker. "You have to stay home."
She'd shut the door in his face.
Shadow would whine.
His whole body would droop like an old mop
as he walked back to the house.

When Samantha came home, Shadow would lick
her face so hard it almost disappeared.
Sometimes, Samantha would push him away.
"Wet," she'd say.

One afternoon, a boy named Tommy
came to play.
Samantha and Tommy made towers
out of blocks.
When Shadow tried to help,
the blocks fell down.

"Bad Shadow," said Samantha.
She hit him on the nose.

Shadow went to his bed and lay down.
When Mrs. Parker called him for dinner,
he didn't get up.
When Mr. Parker brought him a bowl
of water, he didn't drink it.

SHADOW

Samantha went over to Shadow's bed.
She patted his paws.
"Bye-bye," she said.
She was going to her grandparents'
for the weekend.
Shadow wagged his tail once, but he didn't move.
He lay on his bed all weekend.

"Something's the matter with Shadow,"
said Mr. Parker.
He took Shadow to the vet.
But the vet couldn't find
anything wrong.

"Maybe something's bothering him,"
said Mrs. Parker.
"I think I know what it is.
I'll be back later."
Mrs. Parker was gone a long time.

When she came back,
she was carrying a basket.
The basket wiggled.
Mrs. Parker opened it...
and a puppy leaped out!
"Shadow needs his own baby,"
said Mrs. Parker.

Shadow jumped up and down like a yo-yo.
He ran over and smelled the puppy.
Its little body was as warm as wool.
Shadow licked its face.
It was as fuzzy as a teddy bear.
"We'll name him Sam," said Mrs. Parker.

Shadow had to teach Sam
not to chew up Mrs. Parker's
running shoes.

Or Mr. Parker's tennis balls.

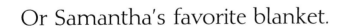

Or Samantha's favorite blanket.

He had to teach Sam to come
when he was called.
And he had to play with him
all day long. The puppy kept
Shadow *very* busy.
But Shadow was happy.
Now he had two babies...

And so did Samantha!